INFERNO

A Gryphon Series Resurrection Novella
Written by
Stacey Rourke

Cover Design by Broken Arrow Book Covers
Editing & Proofing by There for You Editing, Melanie Williams, and Cheree Castellanos

Other Books by Stacey Rourke:

THE GRYPHON SERIES:
The Conduit
Embrace
Sacrifice
Ascension
Descent

The Legends Saga:
Crane
Raven
Steam

Reel Romance:
Adapted for Film
Turn Tables coming soon!

CHAPTER ONE

Hands on my knees, I retched into a nearby bush for the third time since I began my journey. Over half my life had been spent in a hell dimension, during which I witnessed some *truly* gruesome atrocities. Even so, I had to doubt anything would ever haunt me the way the bone-grinding crunch of Gabe Garrett's spine snapping did. In the moment of the strike, his stare locked with mine. I watched the shock of pain widen the whites of his eyes before the light of life flickered out. Nothing but a snuffed out future remained.

He was a good man.

He was to be a father.

Now, only from the Spirit Plane would he gaze upon his child's sweet face.

Having fought beside the eldest Garrett, and eventually coming to call him a friend, I couldn't let the details of his disappearance become an unsolved mystery to his family. They deserved to know. *She* deserved the truth.

Stretching out my hunched back, I wiped at my mouth with the back of my hand. Celeste's dorm sat only a parking lot and a quad away. For normal people, running into an ex could prove to a tortuously awkward situation. Celeste and I? We were about to elevate that bar to a whole new level.

Our relationship defied labels. I was sent to execute her. She learned the truth and responded with a violent rebuttal. I, however, became a demonic traitor just to fight by her side, resulting in her feeling the need to protect me by casting me to the Spirit Plane. Somehow, we found our way back to each other. And, amid all of that, we fell in love. I took a knee before her and offered her my forever. Sonnets are written about the kind of bond we shared ... and the occasional naughty limerick.

If this were a fairy tale, our happily ever after would have followed in a swell of music and lift of doves.

But, my girl, she's a hero. In the face of the greatest battle we ever encountered, she sacrificed herself to save us all. Rowan and I both followed her to the Spirit Plane, pleading for the Gryphon to spare her.

Out of affection for his Conduit, he agreed—with strict terms.

All of us were brought back, all given normal lives. In exchange, anything supernatural was wiped from our memories, including every moment of our time together.

The truth of it? They could erase my mind, but they couldn't touch the scar of her name burned onto my heart. *There*, she never left. Not for a moment. I couldn't indulge in another woman, because I knew my heart was spoken for—even if I couldn't remember her face. Compare it to humming a song, when you can't quite remember the words. Its mark has been left on you, while the chords of the chorus float just out of your mind's reach.

Memory restored by Rowan's desperation, the entire symphony of her radiance returned to me.

To her, I was a stranger.

To me, she was everything.

There was a thin line between romantic and creepy, I feared I was Highland dancing right along it.

Proving fate is a cruel mistress with a sadistic sense of humor, the first words I would knowingly speak to her after over six months apart would be of death and gut-wrenching loss. Chances are she would end up hating me. Still, if Celeste could become a gryphon to save the world, I could play the clod that knocked on her door to inform her of her brother's fate. It was a paltry sacrifice in comparison.

In my mind, the soundtrack of breaking bone played on a loop once more.

Squeezing my eyes shut, I swallowed hard to force the memory away. Filling my lungs with a last minute calming breath, I aligned myself to the task ahead.

Three strides, that's how far I made it.

My detour came in the form of a body propelling off a nearby sapling. Feet collided with my ribs, forcing the air from my lungs in a pained huff. Stumbling to regain my footing, my hands curled into tight fists at my sides. The demon within tittered his giddy delight at the prospect of stretching his legs for the first time in months. Assuming a wide-legged stance, I struggled to keep my dark, less than personable side at bay. He doesn't play well with others.

Terin, the Conduit of the Phoenix, landed in an easy crouch in front of me. Flames licked viciously in the pools of her gaze.

"Caleb," she hissed, the threat in her voice sizzling like live fire. "It's been a while."

Shoulders relaxing to the slightest degree, I greeted her with a brief nod. "Terin, glad tah see ya in the driver's seat of ye'r own vessel. When did ya'r memory return?"

A low rumble seeping between her bared teeth, Terin launched for me in a tornadic fury of flying fists. She didn't pack quite the wallop Celeste did. Still, pit her against the toughest, human MMA fighter and my money would've been on the fiery redhead.

"My sensei awakened me with *all* the knowledge I lost." Jab, jab, cross elbow, knee kick: thankfully my reflexes allowed me to block and dodge each while barely breaking a sweat. If she channeled her inner Phoenix and turned up the heat, that would be an entirely different matter. "That includes my calling. I know all too well what I am now."

Forearms raised, I shielded my face from her onslaught, taking a few body blows in the process. "Did he ... *umph* ... tag on that I'm on ya'r side now? Have been ... whoa, there ... for a while now. My place on the white hat crew has been firmly established."

Corkscrewing into a backspin, her elbow cracked into my chin hard enough to snap my head back. "I am aware," she stated quite calmly for someone unleashing all of hell's fury. "All the details for this little melodrama returned to me while some random rugby player had his tongue shoved down my throat. Including the fact that you are on your way to disrupt the Garretts, which I cannot allow."

Sweeping her strike in a low block, my lips screwed to the side. "I don't mean tah alarm ya, but ya may be the first woman *ever* to gain wisdom in the arms of a rugby player. I have tah ask, lass, could this whole onslaught be because ya can't get the taste of frat boy and bad decisions out of yar mouth?"

Planting her feet, she stabbed her fists onto her hips. "*Hey*! No slut shaming! Even if my human alter ego *did* seem to be going for some sort of record."

Seemingly ticking through the mental roster of her conquests, Terin's face morphed from annoyance, to disgust, to blind screaming rage. Pivoting on the ball of her foot, she hammered me with a series of roundhouse kicks, followed by a spinning back wheel-kick.

I dipped into a low crouch, narrowly missing getting my clock cleaned by the side of her foot. "Can I ask why we are doin' this? Is that allowed?"

"Because," forcing the words through gritted teeth, she unleashed a series of body blows meant to tenderize my ribs, "my human self was looking for a release that only a solid spot of violence can relieve. And you, my sinewy leprechaun, are the perfect partner."

"You're not even goin' tah buy me dinner before I scratch that most intimate itch for ya?" Catching her wrist, I granted myself a momentary reprieve from her onslaught, only to be yanked in to a hook kick to the back of the head.

A couple—wearing oversized garments that looked desperate for a wash—moseyed passed. Gazing our way with red rimmed eyes, they nodded their appreciation.

"Our school has the best theater department," the mate with the man-bun marveled with audible awe, a cloud of Patchouli oil permeating off of him.

Nodding her agreement, his girlfriend's dreadlocks bobbed along. "They're so committed to their art."

Guiltily dropping our hands to our sides, we watched them leave in an uncomfortable moment of silence.

The second they were safely out of earshot, Terin cocked one hip and peered my way with annoyance. "You know, when you say things like that, you sound just like Rowan."

Raising my palms to halt any further attacks, I let my shoulders rise and fall in a casual shrug. "Well, I did spend a few centuries with the bloke. Speakin' of, am I to guess ya'r sudden mystical resurrection had tah do with our boy getting his soul swirled in evil with a dollop of malicious mutt on top?"

Shaking out her arms, Terin inspected a knuckle she'd split open, most likely on my face. "Colorful description, the human lingo seems to be rubbing off on you. Yes, Rowan is the main objective, but today *you* were the mandatory target."

Clucking my tongue against the roof of my mouth, I dragged my fingers through my hair. "Ay, I was goin' tah see Celeste. It would seem the Council is worried about the lingerin' connection between us."

Terin blinked my way, face white-washed of emotion. "*Gross.* The Council has more important issues to concern itself with than your pelvic magnetism for each other."

"And yet, here ya are," I pointed out. Weaving my hands behind my neck, I stretched out my back which had taken a few solid strikes during our rumble.

Lips pursed in distain, Terin's head titled. One ginger curl fell into her eyes, and she flicked it away with a toss of her head. "Look, all I know is that the Garretts are exactly where they need to be. *All* of them. I am under strict orders to ensure you leave them be."

"Gabe is dead," I stated flatly, letting my hands fall to my sides. "He was a brave warrior that I had the good fortune tah fight beside, and now he's gone. His family has the right tah know he died a hero. I owe them that."

Features softening, Terin dragged her tongue over her lower lip. "You aren't the only one that cares for them. Celeste has become closer than a sister to me. She is more my family than anyone has been in centuries, and—if I am being honest—after seeing her in yoga pants, I've got quite the girl-crush on her. Unfortunately, there is some big, bad mojo going down and we need to keep it *far* away from her *and* her kin. If she gets her memory back, this realm will be lost to her forever. We can't allow the wall of the cloaking spell to crack, Caleb. *You know that.*"

"There's no greater anguish than havin' tah move on without closure." My accent thickened as I acknowledged for the first time the dull ache in my chest that called out for my sassy little brunette. "I can't do that to them. I'll go, tell them what happened and where tah find him, then I'll disappear from their lives. No cloaks will be ruffled, or memories jogged. I need tah do this, Terin. With or without you."

Deep in the pits of her eyes a blaze ignited. Like wildfire it spread, licking over her skin and blowing her hair back in dancing flames.

"And if I say I can't allow that?" she asked, threat sizzling through her tone.

A rolling of my neck and I called water to me, relishing in its cool waves lapping through me. Blue diamonds waved in a hypnotic rhythm up my arms, marking me as her perfect counterpoint. "I'd say ya'r going tah have tah stop me, and you've got me feelin' peckish for a fight."

"Ugh!" With an exasperated groan she extinguished her flames. "Fine! If I show you the Garrett family is perfectly content in their mundane existence, will you leave them be so we can get back to the Hellhound hell-bent on sending us all into a tailspin of pain and darkness?"

"Clevah play on words." Shaking out my arms, I released the water effects into a salty sea breeze that licked off into the night. "Howevah, one of the Garretts is layin' cold in an alley. Tha's a far cry short of the definition of content."

Looking more the annoyed twenty-something than a fated chosen one, Terin rolled her eyes skyward. "But if I *could*?"

Crossing my arms over my chest, flannel sleeve scuffed against flannel sleeve. "We're speakin' purely in fairy tale hypotheticals then? Sure. Show me everythin' in her world is right as rain, and I will refrain from knockin' on her door."

"Fantastic! Way to be a team player. Come with me." Terin jerked her head in motion for me to follow. Spinning on her heel, she marched off, her stare scouring the trees that lined the sidewalk.

Expelling an exasperated breath through pursed lips, I fell into step behind her. "I'm only gonna play along with this ruse fer so long, Phoenix. As ya mentioned, time *is* of the essence."

She came to an abrupt stop in front a towering oak whose leaves were tinged at the tips by autumn's touch. Glancing from the treetop to the building across the street, and back again, Terin nodded her approval. "This won't take long. Up you go; defy gravity." With a casual flick of her wrist, she directed me up the tree.

Eyebrows raised, I inspected our leafy destination. "I'm afraid I'm gonna need a bit more information tah go on here, lass."

"It's a line from a hit Broadway musical. Get out of the pub once in a while and take in a little culture."

Dragging my tongue over my top teeth, I took a silent beat. "I meant the tree, pet."

As she combed her fingers through her hair, Terin's curly strands leapt from her scalp in a messy disarray. "Wow, okay. If all demons need things spelled out to them in this much detail, the Spirit Plane is putting way too much effort into thwarting your kind." Clapping her hands together, she addressed me with the wide smile and small words of a preschool teacher speaking to a class of young, simple minds. "Celeste's dorm room is across the street. I know because it's my room, too. See that pink thing hanging from the curtain rod? That's my bra—it's too delicate for the dryer. If you go up this tree, you can look into her room, and see her. 'Kay? Now, ups-a-daisy!"

Brow pinched, I waited for the punchline. "Our master plan is tah be a Peepin' Tom?"

Waving to a group of girls sauntering to the library, Terin fixed a smile on her face that came nowhere near reaching her eyes. "It's the only way to get what you want without causing any unnecessary trouble. Stop making it weird and do that demonic *poof* trick to whisk us up there."

"Well, now I know ya'r messin' with me," I snorted, looping my thumbs in my front pockets. "You could fly yarself up there, easy as ya please."

For a beat she stared, blinking in my direction. "Did you actually *go* to any classes while you were here on campus? I am a *Phoenix*. I can only fly when I go full-on flame. Leaves and fire tend to like each other *a little too much*, and setting the campus ablaze isn't really conducive to the incognito angle we are shooting for. You pickin' up what I'm layin' down here, hot stuff?"

Dropping my chin to my chest, I peered up at her from under my raven brow. "Ya know, I think I liked ya bettah before the influence of modern pop culture tainted ya with the gift of sarcasm."

Terin stepped closer to the tree trunk, tilting her head in one direction and then the other in search of an acceptable perch. "Yeah, well, I liked you better when you weren't crippled by your need to make goo-goo eyes at my bestie. Third branch up on the left could hold us both easily." Craning her neck to glance over her shoulder, she peered my way with a taunting half-smile. "What do you say? You ready to see if she still lives up to that glorified pedestal you placed her on now that you know a pirate pillaged her bootie?"

"Her bootie is living in an alternate reality," I grumbled, hearing the audible pout in my own tone and hating myself for it. "It doesn't know what it's doing."

Before she could argue to the contrary—leaving me no option but to douse the Phoenix in water just to shut her up—I encircled my hand around her wrist and whisked us both up the trunk of the tree in a rolling cloud of black smoke. Familiar with the disorienting rush of solidifying, I called on the wind to draw each floating wisp of our combined entities in tight. The moment Terin's frame shimmered corporeal, I caught her by the waist and steadied her on the branch. Still, she did involuntary windmill arms. Having traveled with passengers many times before, I expected nothing less.

"Whoa!" Fingernails digging halfmoons into my forearm, she seized my arm with one hand and the branch with the other. "I take back every snide comment I made. *Please, don't let go!*"

Pinching my lips together to squash a chuckle, I swallowed down my amusement before pointing out the obvious. "Isn't yar sacred callin' that of a mythical bird? I didn't anticipate heights bein' an issue."

"Heights aren't the problem!" she squawked, burrowing her nails deeper into my flesh. "Plummeting from them is! Wings out here would take this tree out in a fiery blaze, and that ground would sneak up on us *real* quick!"

I would like to say I was still listening, or that I took some measure to calm the panicked heroine beside me. Neither was true. Our perch provided the perfect vantage point … one I quickly lost myself in.

There she sat.

On her bed with her back to the wall, Celeste's knees were drawn up to act as a makeshift easel for the sketch pad balanced on her lap. Her hair was twisted up in a messy bun, held in place by one of her art pencils. Gnawing on her lower lip, she used the side of her hand to mute the line she drew.

My heart lurched in my chest. More than I ever wanted anything in my life, I longed for her to turn the intensity of her gaze my way, if only for a second. Just one more time. There was so much I wanted to say, so many poetic words scripted on my soul. With one glance I was convinced she would see it all.

Circumstance forced a chasm of distance between us. How I yearned to steal a few moments back at the beginning, when I could bring color to Celeste's cheeks simply by brushing her hair behind her ear. Whatever it took, when this was over and the darkness rescinded to the shadows once more, I would get us back to that magical place.

Pausing her creation, Celeste's lead-smudged hand plucked her phone off the mattress beside her. Clicking it to life, she frowned down at the device. Bothered by Rowan's silence, perhaps? Or Gabe's?

I wasn't the only one who picked up on the budding artist's shift in mood. Blonde hair bobbed into the window frame, momentarily blocking my view as Kendall plopped on the bed beside her sister. Clutching her stuffed zebra in front of her, the youngest Garrett adopted a silly mug and made her plush friend dance in front of Celeste's face. Laughing, Celeste playfully swatted it away.

Their Grams sat on Terin's bed, painting her nails a shade of pink so bright I guessed it to be visible from space. When I scanned the room further, the chilly hand of reality tiptoed down each of my vertebrates. Alaina, Gabe's clueless widow, swiveled side to side in the desk chair; the fabric of her shirt stretched taut over her swollen belly. Crochet needles clicked away, creating sunshine yellow baby booties with each methodic sway. Her face radiated with maternal peace. In my head, I could hear her humming a sweet and soothing lullaby.

Guilt seized my throat in a strangle hold and squeezed tight. "She needs to know the truth. To have time to mourn before—"

"She devours that bucket of chicken?" Terin interrupted, referencing the white and red bucket tucked under Alaina's arm that the very pregnant ex-Spirit Guide paused to graze on with ravenous bites. "Yes, I completely agree she should be warned about the sodium content. Can we say cankles?"

"Don't make light of this!" I snapped, the branch creaking beneath my weight as I shifted.

"Or you'll take us both down in a shower of splinters and kindling? Noted."

Head whipping in her direction, my top lip curled from my teeth. "They sit there simmering in their own ignorance! They deserve to know the truth!"

Taking her chances on trusting her own balance, Terin raised both hands palms out. "Take a look at yourself, Caleb. This is why knocking on the door would have been a bad idea."

Glancing down at my arms, I watched black venom seep through my veins, bulging them to the surface like fat leaches. I could feel the sickening cracks and pops of my features widening with my demonic change. It had been too long since I felt that malicious rush … that pull to chaos. Rolling my neck, I fought for control. With my hands glued to my sides, I ground my teeth to the point of pain. It took every ounce of willpower I had to suppress the beast within that roared its desire to seize Terin by the hair and shake her like a rag doll until the truth fell from her lips.

"Gabe died for all of them," I hissed the words through clenched teeth, nostrils flaring with rage. My hand shot out of its own accord, seizing her by the throat. *"His sacrifice can't be for nothing."*

"It's not," Terin stated with deadly calm resolve. Glowering my way with fiery intensity, her body temperature rose to scorching beneath my grip. "I have been assured that each and every one of the Garretts are *exactly* where they need to be."

"And where is that?"

"I don't know!" Flames flared over her cheekbones, igniting her skin to the red flash of day break. "I wasn't privy to that information. But I do know that they have a plan in place, *and* that if you don't take your hand off me *right now,* I will go super-volcano and take you with me."

The branch began to groan and sag beneath us, her heat comprising its strength.

"Swear tah me she isn't in danger!" I demanded.

"I can't do that. I guess you're going to have to trust the powers that be," the steaming Phoenix gasped beneath my grasp. "Take a look at her, Caleb. Does she look like she's in danger to you?"

Seething, I forced my stare back to the window. Celeste lounged on the bed, munching on a drumstick she stole from Alaina. A smile playing across her lips, she said something to Kendall that made the youngest Garrett pounce on her. Yanking the hood of Celeste's sweatshirt up, Kendall tugged the drawstrings out as far as they would go. Only her mouth and nose visible, Celeste laughed along with the rest of the family and tore another hunk of chicken off the bone.

Sails falling slack from my gusts of fury, I wavered. Even I heard the lack of conviction in my tone. "She needs to know. She needs …"

"You?" Terin softly injected rational thought into my vein of absurdity. Grasping my hand, she uncurled my death grip on her trachea. "Are you sure it isn't the other way around?"

Sucking in a shocked breath, I eyed my own hand as if it had betrayed me. Shoving off the branch, I fell to the ground, landing in a crouch.

Terin plummeted down beside me, colliding with the earth in a jarring thump that left her rattled.

"If anything happens to her because of this, I will kill you." Growling the words at the pavement, I granted her only a sideways glance.

The night breeze coaxed her ripened red flame to a soft blushing pink. "If she is put in harm's way, I will storm the gates of the Spirit Plane alongside you."

One brow lifted in question.

Soothing her oversized cardigan into place over her leggings, Terin's shoulders twitched in a noncommittal shrug. "Yes, the star-student is having rebellious thoughts. I blame binge watching *Gilmore Girls* on me forming a deeply rooted need for female solidarity."

"Whate'er the cause, if it works in the favor of our gal, I support it." Pivoting to face her, I clapped my hands before me in preparation of my offering of apology. "A million apologies for that bit of manhandling. My demon hasn't surged in months. It seems he's been hittin' the gym and buildin' strength in his downtime."

"Please," she scoffed. "I'm a Conduit, that was like a warm hug. Although, if I'm being honest, I wouldn't mind you shaking off the veiny, scary look for something a bit more aesthetically pleasing."

"What?" Glancing down at my hands, I found them still to be swollen, enlarged mitts pulsing with tarry demon blood. "Huh … that usually goes away on its own. *Always* in fact."

After twisting her hair into a knot on her head, she held it in place with the hair tie on her wrist. "Well, if it carries on for four hours or more, you should consult your physician."

"I'm serious." Shaking my hands like I was flinging off water, I tried to escape the demonic hold that refused to budge. "This has only happened once before, when …"

I trailed off, unable to form the words.

"When what?" Terin asked, pivoting my way on the ball of her foot. A rogue thought crinkled her nose in disgust. "Wait … you're not transforming into something ickier are you? Because I once fought a Ramoriac demon and their colon drains out their sweat glands. That shit still haunts me—no pun intended."

"This happened once before," I turned in one direction and then other, glancing up and down the street as if anticipating hordes of violent demons to storm the campus, "in a time of war."

"They brutalize your face in times of distress? That seems unfair … whoa! Okay, time for the boundaries talk!" Her argument shifted direction when I did. Grabbing her by the waist, I pulled her to me. Black wisps already roiled around us in a dizzying array.

"There are demons in trouble. Hordes of them. I can feel them. I can track them."

"With some sort of demonic group messaging, you're going to whisk us into the center of the scrimmage? I'm not sure that's the best—"

I didn't let her finish.

Moving us both as a rolling storm cloud, I sought out the thunder.

CHAPTER TWO

Solidifying outside a strip of shops and businesses, I released Terin who stumbled back with her hands on her knees.

The wind lashing her hair around her face, which was tinged green with motion sickness, her gaze traveled the length of the street. "If there is some big demonic throw down going on here, they are keeping it surprisingly low key."

"It's ov'r," I grumbled through my teeth. Finally losing ground, my inner demon retracted its hold. "All I can feel is the stillness of death."

"Traditionally, not a good sign." As she pushed herself off her knees, the low heels of her russet boots clicked against the pavement. Crouching down at the edge of the sidewalk, she peered into the storm drain. "Where did this happen? Underground? Demons like the dark and dank, right?"

"Ya'r profilin', and doin' a poor job of it." With a lift of my chin, I gestured to the coffee shop across the street. The sign on the door, written in newsprint font, read The Daily Grind. A wave of déjà vu whisked me back to the first time Celeste and I met, in a shop similar to that. It couldn't be a coincidence. It felt more like a deliberate step to take me back to the beginning. "Whatev'r happened, it was in there."

Sheer curtains hung over wide windows, allowing light in to the tiny café while denying outsiders like us a glimpse of what had transpired within.

"Aw," Terin tsked, head listing to the side, "that's my favorite coffee shop. They make great scones."

"The bodies aren't even cold yet, Terin. Perhaps we can discuss pastries later?" Steeling my spine, I marched to the door with a determined gait.

Lips pursed, Terin jogged to catch up. "When you say it like that, it sounds cold and callous. I'll have you know I was part of the freshmen initiation committee."

Mid-stride, I shot her a dubious glare.

Dragging her tongue over her lower lip, she hung her head. "Me and a couple other girls liked to be the first to take them to all the local bars. They were like sweet, little drunk babies."

"And ya *haven't* been nominated for a humanitarian award? Tha's the real travesty here." Hand curling around the doorknob, a bell chimed to announce our arrival.

Mangled bodies and the coppery stench of blood welcomed us to a grisly funhouse of someone's maniacal fantasy. Black blood painted the walls in violent slashes. Carcasses draped over tables and slumped back in chairs. Severed limbs were strewn across the floor.

Acidic bile scorched up the back of my throat, my hands instinctively curling into fists at my sides. This was one fight I was *far* too late for.

Shielding her eyes behind my arm, Terin's hand fluttered to her mouth to stifle a heave. "Are they ..."

"There are no humans here," I rasped, sniffing the air. "Every body that fell, every drop of blood spilled belonged to a demon." Emotion muffled my voice to a barely audible whisper. "This was no battle. It was a massacre."

"How can you tell?"

Carefully stepping over the strewn bodies, I ventured farther into the carnage. "Look at their wounds. These weren't caused by weapons. Those are claw marks." I pointed from the torn torso of a lad that looked as though he stepped off the cover of Abercrombie and Fitch only to meet his untimely death, to mauled throat of his curvaceous blonde date. "And someone took great pleasure in rippin' her throat out with their teeth."

"Not someone," a weak voice croaked, "your boy, Rowan."

Forcing my way through the rubble of ravaged flesh, with gore squishing under my boots, I followed the slightest shift of movement. Terin placed her feet in the exact spots mine vacated, matching me step for step. The trail ended at a boulder-sized shifter. His lifeless eyes stared at the ceiling, unblinking. Still, something beneath him wriggled and squirmed.

"I can't look." Terin cringed, yet didn't—or couldn't—avert her gaze. "Is it one of those horse-hair worms? I watched a clip about those. They take over their host and feed off them while they are alive and animated. But the second their host dies, they crawl out of their butt in search of fresh digs. Is that what it is? Demonic butt worm?"

Squatting down, I lifted one limp, tree trunk sized arm. Beneath it, a feminine hand with chipped black polish pawed at the air in search of freedom. "Instead of trapped victim, yar mind went straight tah butt worms. I blame social media. Help me move this monstrous bloke, aye?"

Terin crouched down. Her elbow brushing mine, she shimmied her hands beneath his girth. "On the count of *hernia*, we push." Putting her back into it, she strained against his mass. *"Hernia!"*

Adding my strength to hers, I helped her roll him with both of our faces reddening from the task. "What did this lad shift into?" I mused between gasps. "A rhino?"

One final heave and he slumped onto his side.

A whip thin frame lay crumpled beneath him, and board-straight black hair fanned out around her ashen face, both coated with thick slicks of blood. Heavily made up eyes fluttered open a crack, struggling beneath iron weighted lids.

Placing one hand tenderly between her shoulder blades, I eased Kat—a member of the self-dubbed Misfits of Mayhem—to sitting. Three vicious claw marks sliced across the alabaster skin of her neck, decorating her shirt with tarry gore.

Unweaving the infinity scarf looped around her neck, Terin pressed the fabric to the wounds with a firm but gentle hand. "What happened? Can you remember?"

Kat's mascara smeared eyes rolled back in her head, only snapping back into focus when she winced with the next jolt of pain. "I saw every swipe … heard every scream. Rowan lured us all here, said he wanted to talk about the Conduit. We all swore allegiance to Celeste. We would have gone to the edge of the world for her. Rowan knew that and used it against us. He was the last to arrive … waited for us all to get here before he came in and locked the door behind him." Blood seeped between her teeth, bubbling over her paling lips. "He never said a word—just attacked."

"Lean her forward, gently," Terin demanded. When I obliged, she scooted herself behind Kat to prop her up straighter. "We need to get the bleeding to stop, or we're going to lose her."

"Terin?" I cautiously attempted to interject the full scope of what seemed inevitable.

If the ginger Phoenix heard me, she didn't pause or let on. Easing Kat back against her chest, she cradled the paling demon's head between her palms and guided it to her shoulder. "Sitting her up will slow the bleeding, hopefully long enough for her supernatural healing to kick in. Rowan did a hell of a number on all of them. If this is a Hellhound getting warmed up, I would hate to see his main event."

"Rowan," his name slipped from Kat's blue-kissed lips in a moan, her skin tainted by the gray pallor of death. "I always … had … a … thing … for him." Eyes falling shut, her chest rose and fell one final time.

Eternity's ethereal silence followed.

Defeat sagging her posture, Terin laid her patient to rest on the ground and pulled her leg out from behind her. Offering her help up, I took her blood-stained hand and hoisted her to her feet.

"This makes no sense." Terin chewed on her lower lip, mentally cataloging the scene, her gaze unable to settle anywhere for longer than a second. "Why would Rowan call them here just to kill them? It can't be as simple as hunger and bloodlust, can it?"

Crouching down, I rocked onto the balls of my feet to cross Kat's arms over her chest. "If that's the case, animals are sloppy. That could work in our fav'r."

"*Maaaaasssssssttttter.*"

The noise snaked by so fluently, I thought it to be nothing more than air hissing through the duct work. Terin, however, twitched her head with bird-like interest.

"What was that?"

"I said animals are—"

"Not that." Stepping closer, Terin halted me with one raised hand. "Listen."

The growl of the damned resonated off the walls around us. "*Maaaaster.*"

Pushing off the floor, I sprang to my feet. "*That*, I heard."

As if cued by my alarm, the room writhed to life around us. The walls shook with the menacing vibrato of a chorus of growls rising up in an amplified crescendo. Hunched, mutilated corpses heaved themselves upright. Those whose ravaged limbs couldn't hold their weight dragged themselves closer, their palms slapping against the blood-smeared epoxy floor—vacant slabs of meat, drawn to the only beating hearts in the room. The mountain of a man we rolled over rose onto one knee and matched me in height. From there he swelled, my eyes drifting up, up, up to take in all the towering behemoth.

Sucking air through my teeth, I wagged a taunting finger in his direction. "I'm stickin' with the shape shiftin' rhino idea. Look at the under bite. That thick lower lip is either where his horn emerges, or a sign of bad dental work."

Red eyes glowing from his sockets like a flashing warning sign, his head tipped to glower in my direction.

Steam wafted from Terin's skin, the temperature of the room rising with her agitation. "That's your battle plan then? Poke the bear?"

Matching hungry, red eyes blinked into focus all around us; each of the newly risen abominations adorned with that same ghoulish stare. Their growls shook the shop windows in their frames. Slow and steady they stalked in a tight formation around us, cutting us off from any possible exit. Kat was the last to rise, the behemoth sidestepping to allow her access to their hunting circle. Her tongue teased over the tip of the canine incisors that sprouted from her gums.

"I don't think the bear cares much *what* we do at this point, it's just lookin' fer a spot to sink its teeth. Back to back, then?" Arms raised defensively, I took a small step back and pivoted on the ball of my foot to align us in a better position to keep an eye on all angles of potential attacks.

"I have a theory," Terin stated, panic driving her tone up an octave.

"That Rowan din't bring them here fer a snack, but tah build his pack?" I ventured, brogue thickening as my stress-level rose. My stare swiveled at the snapping jaws creeping ever closer. Hellhound mythology foretold that new pups didn't complete their transformation until they fed. Judging by the looks in the gleaming red pits of their eyes, they were *starved* for phase two.

"I think that's a safe assumption." Flicking her head to the side, Terin's hair ignited into a mass of blazing whips … one of which lashed through my shirt, branding an angry red line into my skin. The pups surrounding us yipped their pleasure at the enticing aroma of my cooked flesh. "Ideas for an exit strategy would be eagerly received right about now. "

"I *could* easily whisk us out of here before one claw swipes our way." Catching Terin's wrist was like gripping a hot radiator. Still, I gritted through the pain and pulled her in close behind me.

"I feel a big *but* coming on."

"*But*, if we leave, these mutts will break out and feast on the town. I'm guessin' yar hero instincts could ne'er allow such a thing."

"*Ugh*, friggin' conscience," she grumbled. "Okay, then, Plan B."

Heat rolled off of her, the magnitude of it calling forth my own fire. Fingers of flame curled across our arms and shoulders, forcing the horde back a few stunned steps.

Slowly, Terin turned her face to mine. Intermingling waves of blue, yellow, and orange shimmered over her skin. No longer was she a girl on fire. Now, she *was* the flame. Little more than hints of her features could be made out from within the crackling blaze that consumed her.

"How much heat can you take?" she asked in way of warning.

"Never tested it," I admitted, focused on the hound fumbling with the locked backdoor. One arm dangling by little more than tendons, his good hand slapped and pawed in search of the sweet click of that lock.

Terin's gaze followed mine, her surging red flames licking ever higher. "Then, I suggest you run … or brace yourself."

In place of an answer, I grasped her hand harder still. My skin cracked to arid embers at the scorching contact.

A brief nod of acknowledgement and Terin's head fell back. Unfurrowing her fiery wings, she stretched them out in a wide arch behind her. With a roar tearing from her throat, she unleashed holy hell on the unsuspecting coffee shop.

The ravenous appetite of her inferno consumed us all in the fat belly of her geyser. Streamers of red and orange licked and bit over flesh and furniture alike. The stifling stench of burnt hair filled the smoky air. Tortured yelps and howls bellowed their grief to the moon. Ceiling rafters cracked, kindling rained down.

With each breath, I inhaled flames that stabbed into my esophagus and scorched me from the inside out. Throat charred raw, my lungs ached with each expansion. Head spinning, control over my own fire falling me under her blaze, my fingers slipped from her wrist. The floor rose to meet me, my knees slamming into smoldering embers. Vision blurred with tears from the thick smoke, I toppled sideways. My skull found the ground with a muted thump.

Terin's face swam before me, every inch of her painted the pallet of sunrise on a cloudless day.

"*Caleb*?" she ventured, her voice a muted murmur that echoed down to me. Rolling on to my back, I gaped up at her. She reigned over me as the all-powerful goddess she was. Fire, her willing servant, licked over her curves in a promise of submission. "*I can't stop. Not yet. Please, hold on just a little longer.*"

Air leaving my lungs in agonizing, labored pants, my head lolled to the side. Through a haze of detachment I watched Terin turn her back to me and unleash a second wave of her flaming fury. The shop brightened to a blinding eclipse. Granting my cracked and blistered lids mercy, I let them slide closed and welcomed the spiral that whisked me into nothingness.

There, in the abyss, heaven awaited.

The sun's rays were softened by a light Caribbean breeze.

Guitar on my lap, I strummed a soothing melody only to be distracted by the tempting view of the landscape. Celeste sat opposite me, a small campfire crackling between us. Eyes closed, her head tipped back, the gentle wind tossing her hair back from her face.

Pressing my palm to the strings, I paused. No notes strung together could ever hope to capture the radiance that emanated from her and her beautifully pure soul. She owned my heart from the moment I admitted my feelings by uttering those three powerful little words that could change fate and start wars. I wanted nothing more from the future than a blissful, mundane existence filled with Sunday mornings tangled up in the sheets.

"It's not time yet, Cal." Celeste's sweet trill snapped me from reverie. Palm trees swayed behind her in trepidation of the low-hanging storm clouds rolling in. Curling her knees under her, she graced me with a warm smile tinged by sadness. "Our aisle to that fated ever after will be painted with blood and lined with bones. There will be time for soulful serenades and stolen glances when the last of the hell-fires have been snuffed out." Toes wriggling in the sand, she rose to her feet and closed the distance between us. Positioning a foot on either side of my hips, she sank onto my lap with a seductive little wiggle. Lips teasing over mine, her voice dropped to a throaty whisper. "We could ascend together and rule our kingdom side-by-side, or spend eternity rotting in a cozy little tomb for two. Whichever way the pendulum falls, fate has aligned our destinies and entwined our hearts. But for now, my succulent Irishman," hand brushing the nape of my neck, she weaved her fingers into my hair and wrenched my head back with enough force to toe the line between pleasure and pain, "I need you to wake up!"

CHAPTER THREE

A light mist caressed my skin, soothing every crack and blister. Cradled in a lush mattress of grass, its earthy aroma eased my scorched lungs with each inhale. A breeze as delicate as an angel's breath softened the sun's beaming rays.

Forcing my heavy lids open, I squinted into the light, blinking hard to focus. Palm trees swayed overhead, blurring the lines between dream and reality. Rolling onto my hip, I groaned at the bark of protest the movement garnered from every inch of my body. Cliffs covered with lush emerald foliage horseshoed the landscape. In the center a white foam waterfall flowed from the rock, bubbling into an otherwise still pond.

A red-haired form crouched ankle deep in the water. Pulling off the remaining rags of her singed and tattered sweater, Terin knotted it around her waist and adjusted the straps of her flesh-colored tank top. Hearing me rustle and moan behind her, she glanced over her alabaster shoulder in my direction, scoffing at the confused scowl etched into my features.

"This is not the Conduit you're looking for," she taunted, waving her hand in Jedi mind-trick fashion.

"What?" I eloquently rasped, pushing myself up on one elbow.

She twisted her hair up in a messy bun, then secured it in place with a hair tie on her wrist. "You were saying our girl's name in your sleep. I wager seeing me when you woke up is a bit of a disappointment."

Taking in the paradise surrounding us with a sweeping gaze, I shook my head. "After that blaze I'm happy tah see *anyone*. I didn't think I was makin' it out of yar wicked bonfire alive."

Dropping her hands, Terin's stare fixed on the bright blooms of wildflowers in the distance, melancholy stealing over her features. "You're the first person that has *ever* survived."

For a moment, neither of us spoke. Words of any kind were drowned out by the ghostly yelps of the pack and the rank smell of their burning flesh that would undoubtedly haunt us both forever.

I pushed myself up to sitting, and pebbles dug into my palms. Tucking one knee under me, I took a few calming breaths to steady the spinning world.

"Ya've done that before," I ventured tentatively, the tone more of a statement than a question.

Her chin dipped in a brief nod. Wetting her lips, she forced her trembling hands onto her hips. "When I first met Celeste, I envied her. Her calling made this powerful, skilled warrior. Mine made me the secret weapon—the nuclear bomb you drop when all else fails. I don't get to select who lives and dies when I unleash. I exterminate, denying myself any explanation or apology. Because if I question it, for even a moment ..." Trailing off, she bit the inside of her cheek and blinked back a wash of tears.

"What I saw back there, what you did, ya'r a—"

"Monster?" she interjected.

Pursing my lips, I corrected, "*A force of nature*. We wouldn't have made it out of there otherwise, and those hounds would've feasted on the entire town usin' the coffee shop as their den."

Eyebrows disappearing into her hairline, Terin plopped down in the grass beside me. "Caffeinated hellbeasts? Espressos between slaughters, and they would've been a global epidemic in a week."

We both managed tight, titters of laughter that rang hollow.

A crane swooped overhead, squawking its displeasure to find us occupying its favorite watering hole.

Rocking on my hip, I lightly bumped her elbow with mine. "Aye, but when ya ignited? *That* was impressive. I've never seen anythin' like that."

She would have appeared coy with her shoulders curled in, if it wasn't for the smug smile tugging at her peach lips. "I remember when I first got my call. My knees shook as my guide led me into the Temple of Magi to introduce me to my sensei. He can take the form of a man, you know. And there, on that scorched mosaic tile, I watched him blaze for the first time." Her face warming in a dream-like trance, her voice lifted to a wistful melody. "He was regal, and scorching. I think that's as close to 'celebrity crush' as I ever got. It was a very confusing time for me."

This time, the laughter that crinkled the corner of my eyes was genuine. "Can I ask ya somethin'?"

"How not all of our clothes burn off when we ignite?" Her fingertips pinched the sleeve of my soot covered T-shirt riddled with holes, and gave it a tug. "Honestly, I have no idea. I think it has to do with layers. Those directly on our skin are safe because of our chemistry. At least that's my guess."

My mouth opened, only to snap shut again. "That wasn't what I was goin' tah say, but it's an excellent question that defies all laws of nature."

"So do we," she countered.

"Touché." Stretching my legs out before me, I leaned back on my palms. "My actual query had tah do with our location. Where exactly we are?"

Terin shifted on her hip, pivoting to face me. "You just *now* got around to asking? That took a surprisingly long time. You're a very trusting individual."

Breathing in the clean, crisp air, I noticed with pleasure that each rise and fall of my chest hurt less than the last. "It's a right paradise. Had I awoken somewhere where apes ruled the world, or monkeys flew about, it would have been the first sentence I uttered."

Terin's face was a question mark of interest.

"Celeste made me watch *Planet of the Apes* and *The Wizard of Oz*," I explained, flicking the hair from my eyes with a toss of my head. "Now every trip tah the zoo I swear I see the primates plottin'."

Turning her head to scratch her ear, Terin tried to hide a rather obvious laugh. "You are a complex individual, Caleb."

"Call me Cal," I suggested, pushing off the ground with a grunt. While my legs wobbled under my weight, I could feel my strength rapidly returning. Turning in a slow circle, I took a guess at the unanswered question, "Rainforests of Brazil?"

"Close." Standing, she brushed the grass from her bum. "Oahu, Hawaii. Your Titan nature is channeled to the elements. I wanted to find a place that could connect you to them as much as possible to aid your healing. This seemed the perfect spot."

"It worked wonders." Peering down at my hands, I turned them over in inspection, flexing and straightening my blemish-free digits.

"Good to know, because I need you at full strength. Side note … we may want to watch the news for sightings of a low flying comet from our flight here."

"*If we can't live together, we're going to die alone*," a familiar voice interrupted, erupting into a fit of snorts and giggles.

"Oh! Oh! I've got one." Thick, waxy brush rustled as a figure emerged from the tree line on the opposite side of the pond. Glancing back at his friends, the bushy-haired newcomer adopted a horrible English accent. "*If you two are done verbally copulating, we should get a move on.*"

"Guys, I think this is it!" Eddie, the makeshift leader of The Dark Army Glee Club, shoved his way passed his friends. "This is the waterfall where Kate and Sawyer …"

Eddie pulled up short. Eyes widening to saucers, he blanched. His pause lasted a nanosecond before he spun on his heel and slapped at his friends to get them to move with frantically flailing arms.

"*See ya in another life, brotha!*" he shouted over his shoulder as he made a desperate attempt at escape.

"Demon to demon, it's just embarrassing." With a sigh, I transported myself directly into his exit path. "Hey ya, boys! Going somewhere?"

Beard Face backhanded Eddie's arm, his lips forming a downward C. "See? If we could still teleport this wouldn't be a problem."

"*Shut up!*" Eddie—dubbed that because of his uncanny resemblance to Eddie Munster—stabbed his fists down at his sides, his declaration bordering on a whine. "*Ix-nay on the eleport-tay.*"

Hawaii got an extra boost of heat as Terin flapped behind us with her fiery wings crackling and blazing their full glory. "Ugh," she scoffed the second her feet settled into the soil. "I thought there was an *actual* threat. If I knew it was these twerps, I would have stayed on the other side of the pond and intimated them with menacing glares."

Shifting his weight from one foot the other, Eddie snorted. "That wouldn't have worked."

Terin lifted one brow and fixed him with a glare that could have shriveled his manhood and eviscerated his soul.

Lone Twin leaned in to whisper in Eddie's ear in a not-so-hushed tone. "That totally works; it made all my outtie parts innies."

One hand on a neighboring sapling, I crossed my feet at the ankles and gave them my best cavalier smile. "What's happenin', lads? Little bit of a holiday in the midst of a new dark force rising?"

Beard Face's prominent Adam's apple bobbed in a deep gulp. "We … uh … came here on a *Lost* tour."

Retracting her wings with a roll of her shoulders, Terin's brow puckered. "A lost tour? You came here to get lost? That actually sounds pretty cool, like an adventure in self-discovery."

"No, not geographically lost." Lone Twin batted at the air between them, as if that was the most ridiculous thing he had ever heard. "*Lost* the TV show! We came to see the locations it was filmed at!"

"That's decidedly less cool." Terin grimaced.

Before they could answer with what would obviously became a mind-numbingly dull debate, I shoved off the tree and stalked closer to the trio. "A better question still is why one among you is missing, and you picked this exact moment to haunt the same forest the smoke monster did."

Eddie stabbed a victorious finger in my direction. "*You watched it!*"

Catching his accusing digit in my fist, I wrenched it back until he whimpered. "Netflix wasn't even a thing during my last bout as a human. I *may* have enjoyed the occasional binge for long enough stretches to hate myself. That does *not* answer the question of your sudden wanderlust."

"*We're hiding! We're hiding!*" Eddie erupted, only to be shushed by his cohorts. "We bound our powers and we're hiding!"

Releasing my grip, I let him fall. His knee slammed into the spongy earth. "You know what Rowan has become. Why would you relinquish your greatest weapons with him on the loose?"

Hooking his friend by the elbow, Beard Face hoisted Eddie to his feet. "We did it *because* Rowan is on the loose."

"*Shhh!*" Lone Twin spat, his face flushing a deep magenta.

The other two immediately clamped their mouths shut, their gazes forced to the ground by the visible sorrow that sharpened their features.

Locking stares with Terin, I noticed a twitch of unease beneath her left eye. If I had to guess, I would wager she felt the same foreboding ripple in the air I did.

"Lads," I pressed, "where's Red? What happened tah your fourth mate?"

Face crumbling in pain, Lone Twin emitted an inhuman squawk in the back of his throat that he attempted to stifle behind his fist.

Eddie clamped a comforting hand on his friend's shoulder.

Beard Face dragged his palm over the back of his neck, chewing on his words as if fearful of the consequences of unleashing them. "Rowan came to the loft and asked us *one* question: who else knew about Celeste."

Terin took a step closer, a bead of sweat trailing down her neck and over her collarbone. "What did you tell him?"

Beard Face wet his parched lips. "Nothing he didn't already know. The only players in this that didn't get the bleach brain treatment were Rowan, the Misfits of Mayhem, and us."

Mention of the misfits injected ice water into my veins. "The misfits are ... dead."

I expected stunned reactions. Their sorrowful nods of acceptance were far more off putting.

"He came after us first," the solo twin hiccupped, tears streaming from his red-rimmed eyes. "Red answered the door, and Rowan caught us all in a web of his mind control the second the lock clicked. He held Red still and made him look him in the eye while he stalked closer. Claws stretched from Rowan's fingers, and ... *hiccup* ... with one slice he cut Red's throat to confetti. Blood sprayed the walls, and Red couldn't even scream. Rowan kept him locked inside himself until he crumbled to the floor."

"His power was in full force, yet the three of ya made it out alive?" Shifting my weight, I looped my thumbs in my front pockets. "Mercy doesn't seem like his strong suit in his current state. Why would he let ya go?"

"He didn't *let* us do anything," Eddie corrected, his tone sharp and clipped. "We were under his thrall as much as Red. He had every intention of going right down the line, picking us off one by one."

Taking a step closer, a twig snapped under Terin's boot. "How did you get out?"

"He was practically hypnotized by the gushing blood," Beard Face bitterly snorted. "He breathed it in like he wanted to taste it. It wasn't hard to tell that his focus was distracted. He could hold *me* there, but he wasn't prepared for my monster. I unleashed—let the beast swell—and Rowan's grip slipped."

"And you ran," Terin filled in.

When Eddie jabbed a thumb in Beard Face's direction, one corner of his mouth screwed to the side. "Eventually, as soon a Gigantor here cleared us a path."

Wiping sweat from my brow with the back of my arm, I asked, "How did he do that?"

Lone Twin lifted his chin, staring off at the swaying treetops with narrowed eyes. "Remember the scene in *Avengers* when Hulk pulverized Loki? Picture that, but with an enormous orange, lumpy dude in a giant diaper."

Terin's lip curled in disgust. "Actually, I think I'd rather not."

"We couldn't risk him coming after us a second time. So …" Catching the collar of his Hawaiian shirt, Eddie peeled the fabric back to reveal blindingly white skin and an angry red scar. Comprised of a cluster of three swirls, each flared out into jagged points that stabbed in opposite directions. "We did our research and marked ourselves with these. These little babies make us nonexistent on Rowan's radar. As far as he knows, we're already dead."

Edging closer, I pinched the fabric between two fingers and pulled it back for further inspection. "It also makes ya completely helpless if he *does* show up, which could get the *real* kinda dead."

"That shouldn't be an issue," smacking my hand away, Eddie took a step back, "as long as we stay far away from *you*. He came for us, and he'll come for you. It's just a matter of time."

As I raked my fingers through my hair, I tried to fit the pieces of this puzzle into place. "He gave me my memory back. Reminded me of Celeste's callin'. Why would he wake me just tah target me?"

"Sport?" Lone Twin shrugged.

Lips pressed in a thin line, I tapped one finger against them. "No. That doesn't make sense. In the moment he let the hound infect him, he was lookin' for a way tah save Gabe. Hell, a way tah save himself. Like us, he needed answers."

"I know where *I* would go if I was looking for answers," Eddie said with a skeevy chuckle, shaking out the front of his shirt like he was overheating.

Lone Twin bumped Eddie's elbow with his. "You'd go there looking for the remote if you weren't scared she'd gnaw your face off just for being there."

Terin glanced from one of us to the next in search of markers rerouting her on this conversational detour. "Where? Who?"

Ignoring her question for more pressing matters, my chest swelled at the looming threat the trio of misfits were hinting at. "Ya can't mean—"

"Malise, the merqueen." Eddie's voice held the dreamy, wistful cadence of idolized puppy love.

Terin's eyebrows disappeared into her hairline. "Mermaids? Now this story has mermaids?"

Jaw clenched, my mouth opened with a pop. "She's an oracle of sorts. Her reign can be traced back tah when dinosaurs roamed the earth. Nothin' happens on the world above or unda the sea without her knowin' about it. She never chooses sides, and that's how she's stayed alive. Rumor has it she's also quite—"

"Hot?"

"Curvaceous?"

"The object of my every waking fantasy, and a few twisted sleeping ones?" the remaining Glee Clubbers offered, one after another.

"*Attractive*," I corrected, cringing at their proposed suggestions. "She also has a reputation for being viciously, *unforgivingly* brutal."

Eddie nodded in emphatic agreement. "I heard she ordered one of her mer to eat his own tailfin when he interrupted her dinner."

"*Why do you say that like it's a good thing*?" Beard Face spun on his friend, aghast at the glimpse into his psyche.

"What? No one likes to be interrupted while they're eating." Eddie let his shoulders rise and fall in a nonchalant shrug.

"We could go tah her lair," I piped up, purposely side-stepping his icky infatuation. "She *has* tah have more information on Hellhounds than we do, which is basically the equivalent tah readin' the back of a cereal box."

"*Can we*?" Terin mock pleaded. "I long to eat my own arm!"

Raising both hands, I pumped the brakes on her rebuff. "We would pay the proper homage and honor her accordingly to stay in her good graces. But, tah be truthful, this may be our best chance."

"To be fed our own limbs," she reiterated, nodding along.

I spun on my heel and stalked a few steps away. Exhaling a lungful of frustration, I gulped down calm resolve and turned back to face her. "Rowan *will* attack again. That's a certainty. Next time he might not stop at demons, and we may not get there in time tah exterminate the problem. We need tah utilize whatever resources we have, no matter their cost."

"Fine," Terin relented, letting her arms fall to her sides. Golden sparks of mischief twinkling in her eyes, she raised one hand. From her palm emerged a grapefruit-sized fireball that hissed and sizzled with malicious intent. "But if she gets combative, I'll reduce her to fish sticks."

"That is so hot," Lone Twin marveled, sniffing at his own humor. "Pun intended."

Plucking a tall blade of grass, I twirled it back and forth between two fingers. "What say ya, boys? Ya've fought on the side of the good guys, and we could use yar help. It wouldn't take much tah singe those bindin' marks from your flesh and unleash ya as the weapons ya truly are."

Leaden silence plunked down in the space between us and wriggled awkwardly.

"I said that out loud, din't I?" I pondered, flicking the tightly twirled blade aside.

Beard Face and Lone Twin glared Eddie's way, prompting him to speak with their vulture-craned necks and white-pressed lips.

"Things were different then!" Eddie blurted, buckling under the pressure of their stares. Shoulders sagging, he glanced my way in defeat. "When we fought with Celeste, we had all the advantages: the Guardian, the Protector, two Conduits, our own abilities, and—in the end—even an army of demons to fight alongside us. Now, we have nothing but the five of us. No offense to either of you, but our sense of self-preservation demands a whole lot more than that. We wish you both the best, we truly do, but we have to sit this one out. Forget you saw us. Forget you *know* us. Go visit the merqueen. See if she has any ideas on how to stop Rowan. If not, I suggest you follow our lead. Hide who you are, hide what you can do, and run before he kills us all."

CHAPTER FOUR

"You know, in all the time that we spent discussing the horrible ways that the merqueen could kill and/or mutilate us, I never once contemplated that we were actually going to have to go *in* the water to meet her." Toes sinking in the sand with each lap of the tide, Terin jabbed her hands on her hips and stared out at Oahu's turquois sea.

"No part of *Mermaid Queen* made ya think we might be takin' a dip?" I countered, one corner of my mouth tugging back in a smirk. The bathwater-warm waves splashing up to my ankles lured me to venture in farther.

"Well," she said with a self-depreciating snort, "of course, it goes without saying. Still, you should have … said."

Palms together, I bent at the waist in a deep bow of apology. "My sincerest apologies, m'lady. It is completely my fault for not specifyin' that the particular mermaids we seek do, indeed, reside in the *water.*"

"There's different kinds of water," she mumbled under her breath. "Is it too much to ask for a shallow pond, or the pool of a five-star resort?"

Running my palm over the rough two-day stubble of my jawline, I tried—unsuccessfully—not to laugh. "If I didn't know better, I'd think ya were scared, Phoenix. Is that an emotion yar capable of?"

Instead of playing along to my goading, Terin's hands fell to her sides. Chin dipping to her chest, she peered up at me from under her lashes. "*Really?* You're surprised the girl *of fire* is averse to water? All dimples and no brains," she *tsk*ed, "that's the *true* tragedy here."

Dragging a hand through my tangled hair, I got a whiff of just how badly I was in need of a shower. "Katniss has nothing on ya, girl on fire, and neither does this meddlesome ocean. We're headed tah a grotto deep within the belly of the sea. You'll be able tah breathe air, with yar hair only getting' mildly mussed by the humidity."

"Yeah, because *that's* my concern," she grumbled. "Not being stuck under the crushing sea with no way to defend myself."

The wind tossed her hair back in a fiery mane, lashing and licking in fingers of mayhem. The late day sunlight darkened the dusting of apricot freckles across her nose and the rise of her cheeks.

Compassion snared my heart in a tight, barbed grip for the diligent warrior. Her reality had recently been restored, just like mine. That reality fights to the death, develops intricate battle plans, and scopes out the means of escape from any situation. And here I was, asking her to follow me blindly into a death pit.

Insensitive clod, party of one, your table is ready.

Pulling my feet from the sand—which held them like tight suction cups—I turned to Terin with my metaphorical hat in hand. "Lass, it's you and me in this. That's it. If ya believe nothin' else, believe I will do everything in my power tah keep ya safe. Mostly because the idea of facin' the shit storm ahead by myself makes my balls retract so deep inside it'll take a dentist to retract them."

In spite of herself, and the white foam licking the tops of her feet, Terin snorted a wry laugh.

"No, really," I rambled, feeding off her reaction, "I am moments away from emittin' a high-pitched squeal that will forever change the way ya look at me. I'm not proud of it, but I think I can keep it in check as long as ya stay within arms' distance at all times."

Head falling back, her barks of laughter serenaded the sinking sun.

"Okay, smart guy," she relented, clapping her hands in front of her, "what's the plan to stay alive?"

The sea called my gaze, yet nowhere in its whitecaps would I find clues of what was to come. "Normally, I would suggest we bring a gift. Unfortunately, time is of the essence and a conk shell from a local gift shop would not be well received. That said, I think we're gonna have tah go by the grace of our charms."

Terin sucked air through her teeth, the tendons of her neck bulging in a dramatic cringe. "*You* do the charm thing. I'm more a brutal honesty and awkward social interactions girl."

"Straight up respect angle it is," I countered. "The moment we get there we take a knee, bow our heads, and do *not* make eye contact. We don't want her tah feel we're challengin' her."

"Don't make eye contact," Terin mumbled each word slowly, weighing them on her tongue. "So, our strategy is to handle this the same way one would encountering a silver back gorilla? Yeah, nothing can go wrong there."

Arms akimbo, I let them fall to my sides with a slap. "We don't have tah do this. I'm sure with a little research we could find anotha way."

Filling her lungs, Terin exhaled through pursed lips and closed the distance between us to offer me her hand. "We don't have time for that. Rowan needs to be stopped before his vicious pup virus spreads. We go now, bow respectfully, find out what we can, and get the hell out of there."

I pulled back, peering down at her extended hand with narrowed, doubting eyes. "And yar *sure* that's what ya want to do?"

Lurching forward, her steaming hand caught my wrist, singeing my arm hair. "Less talking, more moving in a cloud of nauseating smoke. Chop, chop. Before I reconsider and blaze out of here never to be heard from again."

"*Mmmm,*" Malise, the vivacious merqueen, stood before us practically purring in appreciation, "what *have* you brought me?"

Knee pressed to the slippery rock floor of the grotto, I kept my stare cast respectfully downward whilst saying a mental thank you to the powers that be for granting me this small mercy of opportunity. If flashing the dimples and playing up the broody cursed demon angle was going to help us get out of this situation, I was *not* above utilizing my resources.

Chest expanding with a calming breath, I risked a glance up from under my lashes. "All that I am, the entirety of my insignificant bein', I offer to ya in exchange for—"

"Shut up, demon," the queen commanded with a snap of her fingers. She hovered not in front of me, but in a wide-legged stance before Terin. Tales of her beauty had not been misleading. Easily five-foot-ten of supple curves, she waded from the water onto legs that seemed to go on forever. Blonde hair cascaded over her shoulders, parting ever so slightly to hint at her deliciously ample cleavage. Her bra, comprised of sea shells and pearls, clicked in a tittering of applause as she crouched down.

Hooking her index finger under Terin's chin, Malise eased her gaze to her own. "I do enjoy a fiery redhead, and they don't blaze any hotter than you, do they pet?"

Terin's heart-shaped lips trembled, parting to release a nervous squeak completely out of character for the seasoned warrior. "We're really deep down here. I-I can't see daylight at all. Can't smell fresh air. It's moist and dank, and— are the walls closing in? They feel like they're closing in."

Leaning in, the tip of Malise's pert nose nudged Terin's cheek. "Breathe, angelfish. I won't let *anything* harm you here."

Terin pulled back, her wide eyes forgetting to blink. "Please don't eat me."

A sly smile tugged back one corner of Malise's inviting lips. "If I do eat you," she murmured, "it will only be after you beg and plead for it."

Terin's freckled forehead creased with confusion. "Why would I ever ... Oh. *Oh!* That's ... equal parts flattering and frightening."

Malise caught one strand of Terin's silky hair to deliver a firm, yet gentle tug. "All the best things are. It keeps the blood pumping to all the right places with a steady, hypnotic *thump.*"

She made love to that last word as it left her lips, taking her time to spew it forth with orgasmic promise.

"Now," Malise's hungry stare wandered over Terin's curves, "tell me what brought such a lovely offering to the threshold of my abode? It isn't even my birthday."

Stare drifting about twelve inches *south* of the queen's eye level, Terin mumbled dreamily, "For the life of me I can't remember."

"We're here because of a pirate named Rowan Wade," I offered, adjusting to my role as the third-wheel with a heaping dose of amusement. "Have ya heard of him?"

"Ugh," the queen groaned, rocking back on her heels with the enchantment tarnished—at least for the moment. "If you caught something from him, get a shot of penicillin. If he stole your girl, you're now part of a not so elite club. And, if he broke your heart, consider yourself lucky he's out of your life."

"Ya know him, then?" I pressed, heartrate accelerating at the prospect of us being on the right track.

Rising on narrow, bare feet, Malise padded over to the hot spring in the middle of the grotto. After dipping a toe in first, she slowly sank in. Turquoise scales spread up her legs and over her hips the instant she touched the water. She settled in, and the end of her tailfin slapped the surface of the pool as she stretched. "I've known Rowan since he was a randy bilge rat using his mind control to coerce young bar maids into giving up their virtue. I even let him think he had influenced me once ..." The memory curled her lips into a naughty little grin. "That was a fun weekend. Unfortunately, our union didn't end on the best of terms."

Blinking back into focus on the matter at hand, Terin frowned at the news of Rowan's lack of popularity. "Then, he wouldn't have come to you for information?"

Malise's head fell back in a throaty chuckle. "Darling girl, if there's something Rowan wants, he wouldn't let some pesky detail like tarnished emotions stand in his way. He has been known to come sniffing around for information from time to time, despite my attempts to expose fang and scare him off."

Subtly leaning my way, Terin muttered out of the corner of her mouth, "That was a metaphor, right? She doesn't *actually* have fangs?"

"I suppose ya'll find that out during *your* long weekend with her," I deadpanned, not even attempting to ease her mind.

"Bloody Irishman," she grumbled. Righting her posture, she projected her voice for the sake of the lounging royalty. "Have you seen him *recently*?"

Stretching her sun-kissed arm out in front of her, Malise watched water drip from her skin like diamonds. "Child, I'm over three thousand years old. You'll need to be a bit more specific on what you consider *recent*."

"Within the last month," I offered, shifting from one knee to the other.

Squinting at the wall, the queen ventured back through her endless vault of memories. "All the knowledge I possess, and a concrete grasp on the passage of time still evades me. But yes, I believe it wasn't all that long ago that Rowan visited me last. The lovelorn swashbuckler came here looking for tips on how to woo a lass by way of destroying a Hellhound. Of course, that was *before* he ignored my advice to steer clear of the mangy beast altogether and *became* the sodden thing."

Forgetting how crucial decorum was in my desire to stay alive, I bolted upright. *"Ya knew he became the hound and did nothin' to prevent it?"*

Clearing her throat, Terin caught the corner of my shirt and tugged at it to coax me back down.

"I knew the instant it happened," the queen admitted, gaze sharpening with deadly intent. "I felt the energy shift with his transformation. I chose not to do anything, *boy*, because I do not meddle in the affairs of *humans*. One day your kind will be eradicated from the earth as little more than a temporary affliction. I've seen it before and will see it again. I survive by maintaining a healthy distance from self-destructive plagues like yourselves." Casting Terin a sideways glance, she tossed her a playful wink that fell short of beguiling, considering the bitter nature of her subject matter. "With some carnal exceptions, of course."

The pulling at my shirt stopped, and Terin rose to her feet alongside me with an indignant fire burning in her gaze. "That's it then? You, the regal merqueen, will let our kind be wiped out simply for your sake of self-preservation? There went *my* lady boner."

Malise clucked her tongue against the roof of her mouth. "Always the superhero, ready to lay down her life for even the most pitiful cause." Rolling onto her belly, she kicked over the edge of the pool nearest us, resting her elbows on the rock ledge. "Tell me, warrior princess, what is it you want from me?"

Terin lifted one brow in blatant challenge. "For you to prove that you're decent enough to do what's right? That would be a hell of a good start."

Silence fell, only water dripping in the distance to be heard.

Malise dragged her tongue over her top teeth, seemingly weighing her options between murder or the mundane. After a beat, she threw her arms out wide in acceptance. "Okay, my *scorching* little flame. Have it your way. My brain is yours to pick."

Mouth hanging open, Terin spun on me. "I didn't expect to get this far. My mind is blank."

I patted her gently on the back, then walked to the hot spring with moisture squishing under the treads of my boots. Hiking up the cuffs of my jeans, I squatted down close enough to see the shimmer of violet scales that highlighted the tops of the merqueen's cheeks. "Why don't we start with ya tellin' us all about the Hellhound tidbits ya regaled Rowan with durin' his visits."

Folding her hands one on top of the other, she rested her chin between two knuckles and kicked her tail out with a roll of her hips. "I told him basically what I've been implying to you, which is that the Hellhound ailment is a virus you should run and hide from at all costs. It can't be stopped. It can't be cured. It spreads, it mutates, and it consumes everything in its path like wildfire."

While chewing on my lower lip, I dragged my palm over the back of my neck. Humid air clung to me in a thick, stifling blanket. "If this virus—as ya put it—is unstoppable, how did it fall dormant for so long? And why would someone awaken such a thing?"

The humor fizzled from Malise's gaze, replaced by the harsh edges of reality acquired from years of wisdom. "The curse was resurrected by a branding iron infused with the affliction, wielded by one with nothing left to lose."

"*The Countess*," the title of the malicious sorceress, who once ruled my life, left my lips in a barely audible whisper.

Malise nodded her confirmation. "In my opinion, the nobility of your girl's sacrifice is in no way tarnished by the fact that it wasn't a victory in the *purest* sense of the world. The Countess found a way to live on, in a virus as vile as she was."

"You know of Celeste?"

A smirk twisting across her lips, Malise's gaze sharpened with a deadly glint. "The most formidable warrior this generation has ever known? Yes, I am familiar with her work." Ducking around me, she tagged on for Terin's benefit, "No offense, pet."

"I'm a nuclear bomb!" Terin raised her hand in way of an explanation and let it fall to her side.

Raising one finger, I paused to think, tapping the hovering digit against my lips. "Even so, she unleashed it *after* a long dormant period. Meanin' … it's been squelched before. If not, every barista, bank teller, and flight attendant would be a Hellhound and the world would be a far bloodier place."

"Human lore is so frightfully dull," Malice pouted, clicking the point of one fingernail against the smooth slate stone. "Can I interest either of you in a sandwich, instead?"

"I'm not hungry, but thank you," Terin politely declined.

Malise's tongue dragged slowly over her upper lip, ripening her strawberry pucker. "Different kind of sandwich, love."

I didn't have to turn to know a hot blush filled Terin's cheeks, I could feel the heat of it radiating off my back. "I-I'm good," the Phoenix-girl stammered.

Clapping my hands into a prayer pose, I pressed them to my chin. "Can we *please* stay on topic just a *bit* longer."

"Can't be stopped, can't be cured, *can* be passed from one being to another," Malise counted them off on her fingers, snapping to attention when a final element came to her. "Well, there is that whole Wat Rong Khun thing."

Nodding along, my lack of comprehension made me shift direction to a head shake. "If that was English I didn't catch a word of it."

"Wat Rong Khun, otherwise known as the White Temple, is in Chiang Rai, Thailand. It was originally constructed in offering to Buddha." Flicking her hair out behind her, Malise recited the history with bored detachment. "Some time last century an artist bought it and made it his life's work to restore it. The simple fool believes the project is his key to immortality." She snorted her contempt at the simplistic idea.

Footsteps squished up beside me, Terin's shoulders raising with hopeful interest as she neared. "And this artist also happens to be the world's most powerful wizard, who possessed the ability to contain any ravaging beastie? Because that would be swell."

"He thinks his *hammer* is going to help him live forever." Sarcasm slathered Malise's every word, her face white-washed of emotion. "I think it's safe to say he won't be your fix-it guy."

"Then why bring him up?" Quickly losing patience, I bit the inside of my cheek hard enough to taste the coppery rush of blood.

Malise's tone sharpened to a razor's edge. "It's not about *him*. The true magic lies within the temple." Lips pursed, she murmured her appreciation, "Oh, and it is a *vision*. The entire structure is a symphony of bone and ice, every inch a tribute to the raw struggle of the never-ending battle that is life. Along the path that leads to the entrance, four stone hands hold up clay bowls in offering. Three are Buddha bowls that offer hearty food and grains to their god. The fourth, is a Tibetan Singing Bowl."

Grasping at the only element I could finally follow along with, I dipped my head in a jerk of understanding. "They're used tah signal the beginnin' and end of periods of meditation."

"There's a smart boy." Malise's hand snaked up the cuff of my trousers, until an involuntary twitch of my leg caused her to pull away with a throaty chuckle. "The sound is said to clear away negative vibrations, allowing a freshly cleansed chi into the space. The Singing Bowl at Wat Rong Khun is *far* different. Once rung, its hypnotic melody calls to the darkness, luring it in. Of course, greedy little artifact that it is, it doesn't stop there. It takes everything, draining the poor soul its unleashed upon until they are reduced to little more than a helpless babe in a mortal shell."

Rocketing to my feet I passed a small circle in the rocky cavern. "That's it! That's our answer! We use the magic pottery tah suck the evil out of him! I tell ya, ya gotta hand it to the Tibetans—they know good pot! Tibetonians? Tibettites? Ah, it doesn't matter! We're finally on to somethin'!"

"Look how excited he is." Terin turned, watching me over her shoulder. "I see a happy dance coming on."

"He's proving to be a bit premature, as most men do." Malise cupped her hands in the water, pushing back with one wide stroke. "He failed to hear the part where all power is *sucked* from the inflicted. Our boy, Rowan, is currently punch drunk on that power and bloodlust. If he thinks you're plotting *anything,* he will tear out your tongue and wear it like a Yakama."

"Gettin' him there is a matter of geography." I swatted her barb away with a dismissive flick of my wrist. "Batin' or tauntin', that lad has been like a brotha tah me for centuries. I can play on his desires and vices enough tah get him there. What I don't know is how tah use the singin' bowl when I get him there. How does it work?"

Stilling her strokes, Malise bobbed upright in the center of the spring. "The technique is a delicate one, each step more crucial than the last. You must start by playing—"

Her words faltered, brow creasing.

A black shadow torpedoed through the space with predatory focus.

I blinked once, twice, and again to clear my eyes.

A choked gasp seeped from Malise's parted lips.

Her chest exploded outward, filleted flesh bulging and dripping from the gaping cavity.

The merqueen's eyes widened to sand dollars. Slowly tipping her head to inspect the wound, blood oozed from the corner of her mouth. One final glance up, with mortality's panic slicing lines of terror across her face, and Malise slumped sideways. She collided with the water like a fallen oak.

Rowan—or a version of him—solidified in front of us with Malise's over-sized heart clutched in his blood-soaked hand. Not so long ago, the time spent on the deck of a ship had kissed his skin to a golden brown and lightened his hair to a gleaming flaxen. Now, darkness tainted every inch of him.

"If I could offer a suggestion for the song-bowl thing," he casually mused, raising a ventricle to his mouth, "I would *love* to hear a chorus of 'Killing Me Softly'."

Curling his lips around the heart chamber, he sucked mouthfuls of pulsating life from the still-twitching muscle, draining it dry with a noisy slurp.

CHAPTER FIVE

"Rowan, this isn't you, mate." Jaw tensed, I risked a tentative step closer.

Flinging the depleted heart aside, Row wiped his mouth on the back of his arm, smearing slashes of ruby gore across his face. Complexion drained bone white, he flicked a strand of hair the color of ash from his black eyes.

"Not me, but not alone." His cheek twitched in manic desperation. The cadence of his voice rose and fell from plaintive whimper to gruff growl. "Protect the girl. *Kill them all.*"

Radiating heat scorched my arm, Terin edging up beside me. "Protect who, Rowan? Celeste?"

His frame convulsed at the mention of her name. Head whipping side to side in inhuman blur, his bones cracked and popped into a muzzle that retracted as quickly as it appeared. The spasm passing, his shoulders slumped, chest rising and falling in fevered pants.

"Don't say her name. *Can't* say her name," he pleaded.

Despite everything, Celeste remained his trigger. Fighting back my instinct of possessive jealousy, I utilized that as the only tool I had to work with. "She wouldn't want any of this. Ya know that. Ya know *her.*"

Eyes bulging to manic saucers, he paced alongside the hot spring where the merqueen's body floated like discarded trash. "Doing it for her. All for her. Sever the line. Destroy the connection."

"Sever the ..." I parroted, chewing on the words. Icy awareness chilled me to the bone. "You're destroying any connection between you and Celeste."

Planting his feet, Rowan spun on me, hands clenched into white knuckle fists at his sides. *"You can't say her name!"* The force of his bellow reddened his face, the tendons of his neck protruding.

Terrin's hands raised to pump the brakes on his hissy fit. "Okay, no problem. We'll go the Rowling route and call her She That Shall Not Be Named. Motion passed, now let's stay calm."

If he heard her, he was too far gone for the words to register. Again, his head shook, morphing outward with each frantic whip. A flash of canine fangs. The blaze of blood red eyes. Ears elongating to points. A widening snout tearing from Rowan's chiseled features. Through the flurry, the beast emerged in all his heaving, nightmarish splendor.

"*Demon,*" he hissed, jaws snapping in ravenous delight. Head snapping in Terin's direction, he tilted his head in a fashion more canine than human.

Sniffing the air, his jaw lolled open, drool dripping from his fangs. "And *the Conduit*. Your delicious scent gives you away, Chosen One. I *longed* to hunt you down, but it seems my generous new host delivered you right to me. What an unexpected treat for fangs and flesh to revel in."

"The Conduit," Terin sampled the phrase, the mistaken identity souring on her tongue. "Yes, I suppose I am."

A sidestep and I positioned myself between her and the hound. "I love ya, brotha. But, I'm not gonna let ya raise one hand tah harm her."

Red eyes bore into me, daring me to attack. "My essence was forged in the pits of hell. My appetite has leveled entire kingdoms. Do you really mean to challenge me, boy?"

Lungs expanding, I called water to me. Blue diamonds ebbed and flowed across my skin. Salty sea air breezed through the cave, tossing my hair from my scalp.

"I've spent my fair share of time in hell." Raising my arms at my sides, the hot spring responded to my call, churning and slapping angrily against the rocks. "Shall we compare monsters? I bet mine's bigger."

The Hellhound stalked a slow circle around us, prompting me to follow his movement to deny him a path to her.

"Wanna take a run at the title of alpha, do you?" His tongue smacked against his teeth. "Ask me nicely and I will keep you alive long enough to watch her die. Her screams could act as your funeral march before I rip out your throat and reveal you for the pitiful little bitch you are."

Chin to my chest, I focused on the water. My rage channeled through it, swelling it from the pool in a furious cyclone. The roar of its lashing winds echoed through cavern. "They say ya can't die," I shouted over the howling storm. "I do hope that means ya'll suffer for all eternity when I cast ya tah Davy Jones' locker."

Fixing his ominous crimson stare my way, a low-rumble of laughter leaked from his clenched jaws. "Such brave posing and posturing. Even so, you've forgotten one crucial detail."

A twitch of his head and an unseen hand closed around my throat, hoisting me up with barely the tips of my toes brushing the ground. Gasping for breath, I lost my hold on the water. It splashed down dormant, jostling the carcass of the floating merqueen.

Prowling intimately close, he whispered against my cheek, "I possess all your friend's talents now. If it suits me, I will bring you to your knees and make you worship me as your messiah."

Flames burst from Terin's shoulders, her hair licking from her scalp in a blaze that ignited the room the bright orange of dawn. "*Let him go!*" she flared.

The hound raised one finger and Terin's mouth knit shut. Weaving between us, he edged alongside her, dragging the back of his knuckle down her cheek. "The things I could do with control of your mind. I could make you offer me your throat and beg me to hurt you just a *little ... bit ... more*."

"*Keep your hands off of her*," I rasped with as much force as I could muster.

Burying his nose in the crook of her neck, the hound breathed deep. "I'm going to explore every inch of you. Indulge my cravings in your flesh. Tell me, Conduit, what you want me to do to you?"

Chin quivering, tears welled in Terin's eyes as her own lips betrayed her by speaking his desires. "I want you to devour me."

Struggling against the force trapping my arms captive at my sides, my shoulders thrashed violently from side to side. "*Terin! Ya will get through this, lass! I promise ya that!*"

The hound turned his gruesome snout my way, strands of his hair tickling Terin's alabaster throat which she held still and stretched in unwilling offering.

"*Tsk, tsk*," his tongue clucked against the roof of his mouth. "Don't lie to the girl. That's simply cruel."

The unseen noose around my neck tightened. Mouth opening and closing in desperate gulps, my ears rang in warning. Black spots danced before my eyes, quickly banding together in a curtain of darkness.

Hand to her throat, the hound guided Terin back, easing her down against a hefty bolder. Tears zigzagged down her cheeks, fear trembling her clamped lips.

"Don't pass out on us yet," the hound encouraged, loosening the grip on my throat to the slightest degree. "I want you to watch. To feel the full weight of your impotence to protect her."

Greedily gulping in what air I could, I prayed it would grant me the clarity to plot a brilliant escape—or lackluster fumbling to freedom. At that point either would do.

Back arching, the hound's hackles rose, his top lip curling from his teeth. Terin stiffened as he bowed his head to her neck. His vicious, curled claws weaved into her hair, wrenching her head to the side to farther expose her delicate flesh.

Voice dropping to a throaty whisper, he dragged his sandpaper tongue up from her collarbone to her jawline. "I'm going to grant you your voice so you can scream for me. Be a good girl, and let me hear every torturous moment. Take me on a journey into your nightmare."

Blinking her indignant rage at the ceiling, Terin forced the words through clenched teeth. "I refuse to grant you the pleasure."

Sliding one hand beneath her, the hound pulled her body to his. "As if you could refuse me *anything*."

With a sickening *thunk*, he unhinged his jaw into a cavernous maw. Terin bristled, her eyes wide with the scream she stifled. Turning his head to the side, the hound sealed his mouth around hers. Chest lurching, her legs twitched for escape from the beast preparing to feast on her soul.

The weight of my own helplessness crushed into me more than the ocean ever could. There was nothing I could do for her. Fortunately, Terin had friends far more powerful than myself.

"*Terin*," I croaked, the strain chaffing my throat raw, "*go nuclear!*"

The hound could stifle *Terin*, but the full inferno of the Phoenix was another matter.

Red-rimmed eyes peering my way, her head jerked in denial. Not that I could blame her. Setting off a fiery explosion in air pocket at the bottom of the ocean wasn't the most desirable course of action. Be that as it may, it was a far less terrifying alternative than letting a Hellhound absorb a Conduit.

Strength grossly depleted, I channeled every remaining ounce I could to beckon fire to me in a sizzling cocoon of protection.

"*Do it!*" I mouthed the words through the flames.

No further prompting was required. Lava surged through her veins, seeping to the surface in a potent backdraft that could revile the deepest pits of hell. Her eyes blinked into belching vats of magma. Her scorching explosion gobbled the oxygen in the grotto, making each breath burn through my lungs.

The hound seemed impervious to the anguish of his boiling flesh. His determined hold never faltered, despite his blackened skin festering and cracking into charred brisket. His hair sizzled and melted, crumbling to ash that rode out on the flames. Well-fed beast that he was, simple flames could not wipe him out as they had his newly made pups. Even as his outside shell burned, fresh pink flesh could be seen between the fissures, knitting him back together.

She was the nuclear explosion, and he was the cockroach fated to endure her fury.

"You know you can't let this happen," a husky female voice croaked from beside me.

Unable to turn my head, my gaze flicked her way out of the corner of my eye.

The merqueen rose from her watery grave on unsteady legs, the far wall of the cavern visible through the hole in her chest. A stream of water gushed from her pallid lips. Once vibrant eyes drained to a lifeless gray. Head bobbing with a bird-like twitch, she sized me up as her only available warrior. "If he takes control of a Conduit's essence, he will be unstoppable. You cannot allow such an atrocity to be unleashed on this realm."

"*Little ... tied ... up*," I managed to rasp as fiery fingers latched onto the queen's arm and burned up her limb.

Unperturbed by her roasting flesh, the queen rolled her eyes skyward. "The limitations of mortals are always so bothersome." The tips of her fingers flickering like birthday candles, she rolled them in my direction, freeing me from Rowan's hold.

Crumbling to my knees, I greedily inhaled the foul air in rapid pants.

"Time is running out." Inch by inch, flames consumed her, searing her corpse to the bone. "You must join the essence of your flame with hers. The strength will be siphoned, the Conduit of the Phoenix protected. There is no other option."

Vision blurring from the smoke-filled air, I blinked her way through tearing eyes. "Who are you?"

Legs crumbling beneath her, the reanimated merqueen fell to her knees. Her gnarled hand reached for me, crisp tendons cracking as she caught my wrist. "I'm someone who has seen enough of the future to fear it."

Amidst the smoke, a vision appeared that caused my heart to lurch in a stutter beat.

Celeste.

My Queen.

My Celtic Warrior.

Her almond-shaped eyes lured me closer. Heart-shaped lips, painted an uncharacteristic red, parted to breathe my name. "*Caleb.*"

Blinking hard, I attempted to clear my deceitful eyes.

Still she remained. Seductively biting her lower lip, her gaze leisurely traveled the length of me. "*Join me, my love. Rule beside me as you were always meant to.*"

Clad in a black leather bomber jacket and matching pants, she sat astride a throne of bone. Legs crossed, human skulls rested beside her scuffed biker boots. One red-gloved hand curled against the armrest. Her opposite hand had been replaced by the vicious talon of an eagle drumming a steady beat against her pedestal throne. Expansive black wings arced out wide behind her, shifting with the graceful roll of her shoulders. Around her mid-section curled a feline tail that matched the wings in their midnight black hue. It coiled in her lap as would a serpent waiting to strike.

Tapping the point of her pink, wriggly tongue to the tip of one bone-crushing incisor, she peered down the bridge of her nose at me. "*Join me, or bow before me, Caleb. Those are your only options.*"

A scream tearing from my lungs, I swiped my free hand at the sinister scene. Disbanding, it wafted away in streamers of smoke.

The queen's body laid slumped on the ground once more. Be that as it may, the effects of her message lingered, acidic bubbles that popped to sizzle their paranoia through my veins.

Pushing off the floor, I dove into the wall of flames. In the midst of the firestorm, I found Terin's limbs falling slack—her listless frame held up only by the hound's clawed hand cradling her in a murderous, lover's embrace. The more of her soul he consumed, the less the fire affected him. His hair grew back in blue flames licking and sparking from his skull.

Orange and red fingers of destruction clawed at the stone walls around us, thirsting for sovereignty. Squinting through the smoke, I heaved myself to my feet and stumbled on. Grinding my teeth to the point of pain, I accepted the fire—welcomed it even—and stretched my hand for Terin's.

One thing I knew with steadfast resolve ... if she died, not only would I lose a friend I vowed to protect, but the vision I saw *would* come to pass. We would be thrust into a world where heroes and saviors could no longer beat back the darkness, because they themselves were the things that went bump in the night.

Feeling I offered little more than a sparkler in the middle of a bonfire, I blasted my own flames to the full extent of my capabilities and linked my fingers with Terin's smoldering digits.

An unassuming connection, a desperate touch, and our world detonated. A geyser of flame pounded against the slate ceiling, sending fragments of rock raining down. Stone creaked in protest as our gushing fountain bore through solid stone with the ease of softened butter. Water dripped from the compromised structure, warning us all of the crushing sea that eagerly awaited the chance to swallow us whole. Could I switch from flame to water fast enough to save myself? Such trivial details failed to matter. If I never made it out of that grotto, it would mean I died protecting Celeste.

It was a noble sacrifice I would gladly make.

Pain and torture being old friends of mine, my concentrated focus allowed me to feel shockingly little in the thralls of those fiery fronds. Casting my stare skyward, I watched the deteriorating rock with awestruck wonder. A volcano was rumbling deep within the earth's core, tearing stone layers to ribbons as it scratched for the freedom to spew forth from the captivity of its prison. Terin and I acted as the catalyst for the inferno that reduced rock to ash, allowing veins of blue from the heavy body above to bulge through. The stark contrast of the bold colors acted as an artistic symphony of nature's most violent and temperamental elements. Those sparking orange appendages dug farther still, prying the slate apart despite its screeching objections. The moment the first hole cracked open, I swore I was staring into the face of heaven. A golden ring of fire encircled a brilliant jewel of the sapphire sea. Sunlight radiated from above, sending glimmering halos beaming down to enchant the scene. This second of peace was the eye of the storm; the hitch of breath before the weight of the world came crashing down. In the stillness of that moment I felt no anger or remorse. No pain or regret. What I thought would be my final thought was one of the simplistic beauty of a life, come full circle to redemption.

In the eternity of a heartbeat, I tipped my face to Terin. The roar of the flames bolstered her fading embers. Acting on animalistic instinct, the hound kept his head bowed to his meal, drinking deep of her soul in noisy slurps. Despite his violent feasting, Terin's leaden lids fluttered open. Our eyes met. Her flaming fingers laced with mine, squeezing in a scorching vise grip. I wouldn't be keeping my promise to keep her safe. For that, I was sorry. Still, as thick ropes of water began to stream down from above, I reveled in the victory of the moment. We would beat back the Hellhound's evil reign with the potent punch of the ocean collapsing down.

Blinking my way, Terin jerked her head in the closest thing she could manage to a nod of acceptance and understanding. Her form—a writhing mass of curling flame—pulsed and lurched upward. Her grip on my hand tightened with enough force to crack bone … had I been human. In that blaze of urgency something passed between us. Its undeniable surge sizzled through my veins, igniting my every pore.

Heat.

Strength.

The valor of a thousand battles fought nobly.

Terin's light diminished while mine burned brighter. Her skin began to redden and blister in the heat for the first time in centuries. Even as her flesh boiled, a comforting blanket of peace drifted over her features. The warrior could rest, her weapon forever sheathed.

Howling his displeasure in the sudden staling of his meal, the hound shoved off her. Spinning in search of the prize evading him—the soul of the Phoenix—his murderous glare locked on me.

"*No! How did you—*" The question was knocked from his lips by the bulk of the sea and hunks of rock fragment roaring in with the strength of a freight train. The beast wearing Rowan's skin was bowled out of sight, tumbling deeper into the belly of the ocean. Terin vanished on a wave, her hand torn from mine. Rammed into a crevice where the rock wall and floor met, the sea pinned me in my solitude. Gulping in a lungful of salt water, my lungs burned with a torturous intensity flames could never match.

As I gazed up at the light shimmering down from above, the last bubbles of air glugged from my lips. Picturing Celeste's loving smile, I closed my eyes.

CHAPTER SIX

Lounging against a canvas beach chair, I enveloped Celeste in the cradle of my arms. All my worries washed away, my body was a warm pool of relaxation. "Celeste, lovey, sit up. I need ya tah look at me."

"Can't sit up," she mumbled, nuzzling against my chest, "my bones have melted into the sand. I am one with the beach now."

A delicate breeze lifted her mahogany strands, tossing them back to tickle my neck.

Over my shoulder, a bright light beckoned. I had somewhere to be and time was growing short. Where it was, I couldn't recall. Even so, I knew it couldn't be put off or delayed.

"Won't take but a moment, pet." With gentle hands, I eased her up, loathing the chill left in her absence. "But I have tah say it now or I fear I won't get another chance."

Begrudgingly sitting up, she glanced back over her shoulder. The strap of her black tank top slipped over her shoulder bone, exposing a bit more tempting skin. "Are you finally going to admit to cracking the screen of my phone? Because I watched you set your guitar down on it, and I know it was you."

Catching a loose strand of her dancing hair, I brushed it behind her ear then let the tips of my fingers trail down her jawline to the point of her chin. "It's something more than that, lovey. Although I will admit that yar infernal little device did prove tah be shockingly delicate."

The narrowing of her eyes couldn't hide the humor behind them as she jabbed an accusing finger at my chest. "I knew it."

Catching that outstretched finger, I brought it to my lips to brush a tender kiss to her knuckle. "I need ya tah know that there is nothing I want more than tah spend the rest of my life lovin' ya. Unfortunately, life doesn't always grant us our heart's desire." Weaving my hand around her neck, I pulled her closer. My forehead found hers while her molasses eyes searched my face in confusion. "If I can't have ya forever, ya should know that ya've been the one beacon of light in the stormy sea of my life. You are my safe haven. My bliss."

Her hand closed over mine, confusion puckering her brow. "Getting pretty deep there, Cal. Everything okay?"

"It will be now," I assured her, dotting a kiss to the tip of her nose.

That demanding white light swelled behind me, pulsating its incessant reminder time was up.

There was so much I had left to say, yet only one sentiment seemed worthy. Cradling her face between my palms, I breathed the words into her. "I have loved you 'til my dying breath, and beyond."

The white light swelling to consume me, my lips met hers one final time.

"He's coming to. Turn the hose off."

My eyes fluttered open to a blinding light glaring in my eyes. Glancing around, I found myself in a room comprised of stark white walls, stainless steel medical equipment, and the stench of antiseptic. Four bodies buzzed around me draped in heavy furs, which was odd considering the stifling temperature of the space.

A face swam above me, porcelain pale features contrasted by glowing avian eyes. "Caleb? Do you know where you are? Or what happened?"

Swallowing awoke a burning sensation in my throat that throbbed straight into my lungs. It brought with it the memories of all that occurred. "I … died," I rasped, wincing at the harsh squeak of metal wheels rolling closer. "Is this hell? Purgatory?"

Across the room, someone clucked their tongue against the roof of their mouth. "See," a familiar voice stated, "I told you that you shouldn't be the first one he sees. Your face is all judgement and loathing. You're not a people person, Cassia."

The woman leaning over me, now identified as Cassia, crinkled her narrow beak of a nose in disdain. "And here I was simply trying to spare him the jarring sight of seeing *you*. How silly of me." Breath haloing her face like the smoke of a dragon, she turned on her heel and marched off.

Feet padded across the floor in my direction. Lifting my head off the pillow, I craned my neck to see. "So, I am dead then," I snorted in bitter understanding, letting my head drop back to the stainless-steel table. "I didn't expect the hereafter tah be so … sterile."

Mouth twining into an impish grin, Terin edged up beside me. Burnished orange curls poked out from beneath a fox-hair hood drawn tight at her chin. "Considering the dire circumstances in which we last met, that *did* seem to be where our story was heading. I can see how you could draw such an assumption. That said, no, we are both very much alive. Well, *you're* alive. I died and got promoted to a position on the Council, but those are all technicalities."

Flicking two fingers, she gestured for me to lift my head. The moment I forced myself up, Terin stuffed a freshly fluffed pillow under my head. The fabric sizzled and crunched the moment I eased my head down on it. "You've been unconscious for four days. We've been looking over you, keeping you safe during your transition. Even so, I'm sure you have some questions. My new tenure grants me the authority to arm you with any information you may need. So, any questions perplexing you, feel free to ask."

Wetting my parched lips, I ticked through my mental laundry list of ponderings before opting for the most obvious issue vexing me. "Uh … why am I naked?"

Lacing her fingers in front of her, Terin deadpanned, "That makes it easier for us to probe you."

I paused to consider that, hitching one brow in mild interest. "Will ya still respect me in the mornin'?"

"Respect *and* adore." Terin's features softened to a smile laced with a maternal warmth. "The *actual* answer can best be explained by demonstration."

Crossing the room, she opened a small mini-fridge to collect a frosty pitcher of ice water. With a determined gait she strode back to my side and dumped the contents of the pitcher on my torso without the benefit of a pause for me to brace myself. I cringed out of instinct, expecting icy needles … and shrinkage. The sizzle and steam of the water making contact with my skin widened my eyes to disbelieving saucers. It boiled and hissed, the bubbles popping and evaporating into fingers of steam as quickly as they formed.

"Well, that introduces a plethora of new questions," I marveled, tipping my head as the last vaporous wisp vanished into nothingness.

"Your clothes keep burning off of you," she explained, setting the empty pitcher on the table beside me. "We have this room set at a nippy thirty-two degrees. Yet, I would wager you would describe it as—"

"Downright balmy," I filled in, taking stock of the medical staff tending to me. Each exhale from my caregivers visibly puffed from their lips. With hands tinged icy blue at the knuckles, they checked my vitals and monitored my stats. In between tasks, they blew on their fingers and ran their hands up and down their frozen arms.

"That's right." Terin bobbed her head in exuberant agreement. "And I would wager it will remain that way until you learn to control your new attributes."

My head thumped back against the stainless-steel exam table, the pillow beneath me exploding into the air in a mushroom cloud of ash. "Attributes?" I coughed, inhaling a mouthful of the floating mess.

Edging closer, Terin stared down with sympathetic understanding. Lifting one hand, she moved as if to stroke my hair, only to quickly retract the wandering appendage. She *was* fire. Was it possible my heat caused her to hesitate?

Lips parting with a pop, her avian eyes fixed on her reflection in the table edge. The words that tumbled from her lips made me wonder if mindreading was a hidden talent of hers. "The Phoenix is a wild beast. Like any such untamed animal, it has two lines of thought when attacked: fight or flight.

Today, he was cornered with only one viable means of escape." Forcing her gaze to meet mine, tears welled in her eyes; the tip of her nose stained pink. "This time, it moved from one willing receptacle … to another."

Mouth hanging open, I stammered to form words my mind couldn't fathom. "Wh-what are you sayin'?" I managed.

I couldn't have wrapped my mind around the concept any quicker if she made finger puppets and acted out each of our parts.

Dragging her tongue over her purple tinted lips, Terin rolled her shoulders, straightening her spine with a regal air. "I'm saying, my dear friend, that *you* are now one of the elite, chosen few. *You* are the Conduit of the Phoenix."

All the languages I spoke fell clear out of my head.

"I … uh … wha … *huh*?" I eloquently countered.

"Look on the bright side!" She shrugged, fox fur tickling across her jawline. "You and Celeste are even more perfect for each other now! Who can understand the struggles and demands of being a chosen one better than your own kind? Granted, all you know of it thus far is that you woke up naked and surrounded by strangers. That said, there is plenty more to it than that and you get the pleasure of exploring all facets of your new calling with the woman you love. It's divine perfection at its finest."

Casting my stare to the white tiles of the ceiling, I felt the lead weight of reality settle on my chest. Its heavy presence made each breath a struggle. "Except, she doesn't know that side of herself anymore. If I were tah allow the wall blockin' that memory tah crack, she would *become* a Gryphon."

"You have to *really* want to see it as a silver lining," Terin grimaced, her voice rising a few uncomfortable notches.

"Add tah that my vision of her gone full Dark Conduit," I continued, ignoring her quip, "and not one part of this seems the least bit reassurin'."

All activity halted. Silence crashed into the room, four set of eyes swinging my way.

"Get out. *Now*," Terin barked to her staff in a tone that left no room for discussion or debate.

They scurried off at her command.

The very moment the door thumped shut behind them, Terin spun on me with wild eyes. "*You had a vision?*"

Pushing off my elbows, I sat up. When my head spun with a hot rush of vertigo, I dropped my chin to chest and filled my lungs with a calming breath. "I can't say for certain that's what it was. I nevah had one before. All I know for certain is that it terrified me tah my very soul."

Her clawed hands rose in front of her like she was resisting the overwhelming urge to grab me and shake me. "I need you to tell me the *exact* details … *immediately!*"

Dragging a hand through my sweat dampened hair, I struggled to recall the particulars. "She was herself, yet completely different. She had traits of the Gryphon—the wings, the talons, the fangs—yet they hadn't consumed her. Not entirely. Not yet. They acted as her weapons—her armor. The world around her burned and smoldered. Death permeated the air. She reigned in the midst of the chaos, perched on high from a throne of the dead."

Crossing one arm over her mid-section, she used the opposite hand to drum a beat against her lower lip with the pads of her fingers. Pacing the length of the room, she swiveled on the ball of her foot each time she changed direction. Her lips moved as she marched, working through the problem without offering me further details of how dire matters had become.

After a beat, she spun in my direction, hands slapping against the fur pelts of her coat with a muffled slap. "There's no time to waste. We *have* to expedite your training. This vision is a blessing of knowledge we cannot ignore."

Swinging my legs over the side of the table, I tucked myself into a bit more concealing posture. "If ya remember the circumstances, oxygen deprivation could be all there is tah blame for my disturbingly vivid dream. There's no need for rash acts. Rowan is lost at the bottom of the sea. The Hellhound virus is—"

"Alive and well," Terin interrupted, talking over me. "Our scouts have confirmed Rowan survived. If we can gather anything from your vision, it's that he longs to reconnect with his little love muffin ..."

"Let's ne'er call her *that* again."

"This is no time to jest, Caleb! He *will* go after her!" A bit of her former flame flared in her irises, blasting me with the urgency of the situation. "Right now, our girl is alone and powerless to protect herself!"

Flames ignited down the length of my arms, my chest swelling with a protective surge. "Yar right, one demonic sightin' and all we've done tah grant her a normal life will be for naught. What do I need tah do?"

"You need to connect with your Spirit Guide. The two of you need to be earth bound and battle ready *immediately*." Crossing to the door, she opened it a crack to address the sentry stationed outside. "Send him in."

"Spirit Guide?" Shaking out my limbs, I tried to extinguish my building blaze that spread across my shoulder blades. "I don't recall you e'er havin' one."

Letting the door fall shut, she backed to the far wall, away from my heat. She yanked a fire extinguisher from the clamp that housed it and held it at the ready. "I was a Phoenix for quite some time, *and* I could control my flame whilst wearing pants. Clearly, you're not there yet, newbie."

Arms falling limp at my sides in frustration, I felt the wandering flames tiptoe down my spine. "I need tah get back, Terin. *Now*. Tell me this guide is good. Tell me they have seen battle and know how tah help me get a grip on these new powers fast."

The door flew open hard enough to bounce on its hinges, air moving through the space in a noisy *whoosh* that snuffed out the fire I couldn't squelch. His hulking frame filled the doorway in a mass of bulging muscles. Earth-toned wings stretched wide behind him in an impressive arc. Casual as could be, he leaned one shoulder against the door jam and hooked his thumbs in the waistband of his linen slacks.

As if I hadn't watched him die mere hours ago …

As if the sound of his spine crunching didn't echo through my mind …

"Yeah, I've seen a battle or two," Gabe Garrett snorted with a wry smirk. "As for the adjusting to powers thing … I'd say I have more experience than most in that department. Wouldn't you?"

Mind spinning in a dizzying carnival ride, my head snapped from Terin to Gabe and back again.

Chuckling at my discomfort, my newly appointed Spirit Guide taunted in the tune of an Offspring song, "And all the girlies say '*He's pretty spry for a dead guy*'."

To be Continued!

About the Author:

*RONE Award Winner for Best YA Paranormal Work of 2012
for Embrace, a Gryphon Series Novel*

Young Adult and Teen Reader voted Author of the Year 2012

*Turning Pages Magazine Winner for Best YA book of 2013
& Best Teen Book of 2013*

Readers' Favorite Silver Medal Winner for Crane 2015

Stacey Rourke is the author of the award-winning YA Gryphon Series, the chillingly suspenseful Legends Saga, and the comedic Reel Romance Series. She lives in Michigan with her husband, two beautiful daughters, and two giant dogs. She loves to travel, has an unhealthy shoe addiction, and considers herself blessed to make a career out of talking to the imaginary people that live in her head.

Visit her at www.staceyrourke.com
http://diaryofasemi-crazyauthor.blogspot.com
Facebook at www.facebook.com/staceyrourkeauthor
or on Twitter or Instagram at @rourkewrites

Printed in Poland
by Amazon Fulfillment
Poland Sp. z o.o., Wrocław